Jolene
Adventures of a Junk Food
Queen

Written by
Alexa Palmer and Catharine Kaufman

Illustrated by
John Martinez and Hayden Mills

Published by

**Palmer&
Kaufman**

Book design and layout by Martha Nichols/aMuse Productions

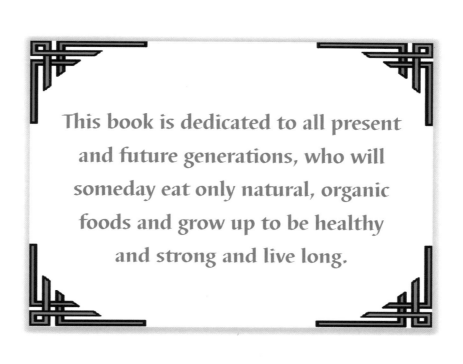

This book is dedicated to all present
and future generations, who will
someday eat only natural, organic
foods and grow up to be healthy
and strong and live long.

J olene loved to pretend. She loved to pretend to be a Junk Food Queen. She dreamed about it each night, and each morning she dressed for school in her favorite junk food. She wore red licorice in her hair, pink taffy underwear, a pair of jelly bean boots, a jean jacket with lollipop hoops, a belt of potato chip loops, a gum drop ring and candy cane earrings.

Jolene's mother screamed at the scene. "Yuckee, take off that junk food, Jolene! It's bad enough you eat it — you don't have to wear it too."

Jolene didn't care. She shrugged her shoulders. She always stood on solid chocolate ground. "I love my junk food," she'd pout. "Inside of me and out, and you can't change that. It's what I'm about."

Then Jolene grabbed her lunch bag full of sweet and sour, salty and spicy junk and ran out the door to catch the big yellow school bus. She was rotten to the candy apple core so most of her friends left her behind. "Get out of my way, Renée," she screeched as she pushed and shoved herself onto the bus. "Let me through — I have the power of sugar and spice and greasy fried rice."

At lunchtime, the healthy Munch Bunch made fun of Jolene. They shouted out, "Even your boogers are made of sugar."

They always said things that made Jolene so mad she turned her back on The Bunch. "You have stinky sugar breath. You must brush with toffee toothpaste. You're the Mean Queen of the Junk Food Scene. Eat better, Jolene, or we won't be your friends anymore!"

Jolene only had one good friend who was sweet to her. His name was Sugar Sam. He shared his lunch with Jolene every day. "I have some chocolate pudding in a dirt cup, and look, Jolene, the dirt is real! Come try some of my wiggly worms."

"Well, only if they're gummies," she spouted out.

Jolene liked Sugar Sam, but she loved his junk food even more. She'd eat his chocolate dirt cup every day. After each spoonful she'd say, "Yummee!"

Sugar Sam looked like Jolene, too. His hair was full of candy coated pretzels, lollipops and fudge. His peanut crunch bars were hooked onto the sides of his overall jeans, and he loved to eat suckers that were bright red and green.

Sugar Sam never ate with Soy Boy. No way! His lunch box was filled with soy burgers, soy milk and roasted soy nuts. He offered Sugar Sam some of his lunch, "Want a bite of my soy burger?"

"I don't eat bad, horrible, hideous, gross, sickening soy," said Sugar Sam as he made a face like he was about to barf, and quickly ran away.

The Munch Bunch tried to change Jolene's junk food ways. "Maybe we could sneak a Granny Smith apple into her lunch box or school desk," they suggested.

Sadly Jolene was stuck in her junk food ways — sugar, salt, grease and goo. Even though her Mom made a "no more junkie snacks at bedtime" rule, she still snuck them under her popcorn pillows.

Jolene found it harder and harder to fall asleep 'cause her junk food junkies made her wiggle and squirm. Then something happened one night that changed her forever.

As Jolene was melting into one of her favorite junk food dreams, floating on clouds of cotton candy, doughnut holes and jelly rolls, a strange mist appeared turning everything into a black licorice cloud above the blue sorbet sky.

Suddenly all the goodies disappeared, and so did her favorite bedtime buddies — Bubba, her chocolate bear, and Taffy, her caramel cat. Crash! Bang! Zap! Jolene bolted, flying onto an empty space, smack in the middle of nowhere.

Jolene started to shiver and shake from the cold ice cream night breeze. She even missed the sugar bugs that crawled from her scraps of bedtime snacks to snuggle up close to her.

Now as the dark clouds began to rise, a tall, skinny man wearing a colorful cowboy hat and fruit leather chaps stood high above the plains. His stainless steel smile sparkled as she stared at his mouth full of metal.

"Who are you?" Jolene asked.

"Well, howdy, Jolene. I'm The Cavity Ranger. You can call me Mr. C.R. — I've been watching you from afar."

Jolene looked down at The Cavity Ranger's gold and silver cowboy boots.

"I've come to warn you about your rotting teeth," said The Cavity Ranger.

Jolene's eyes grew bigger than a pair of giant peppermint patties. The
Cavity Ranger perched his shiny boot on a jagged piece of shimmering rock candy. "I'm here on a mission to save your terrible teeth, Jolene."

"Save my terrible teeth? What does that mean?" wondered Jolene.

"You don't want to be zapped by my big burning drill or spend recess in Cavity Land," said The Cavity Ranger as he pointed his buzzing drill in a whirling spin. "Look out at this desert range, Jolene. It's dotted with dead teeth. Some are studded in sterling like little twinkling stars. You must eat better, Jolene, or your teeth will land here."

She glared back at The Cavity Ranger. "Okay, okay, I'll eat better, Mr. C.R., but I'm feeling cold and strange. I gotta get off this Range."

Suddenly Jolene stared over her shoulder where there stood a great white mountain that seemed to climb up to the sky. "What's that?"

The Cavity Ranger's drill was spitting sparks of fire as he aimed it at Marshmallow Mountain. "Many people have tried to climb those pillow peaks, but it's a tricky trick with stuff that sticks."

Jolene had two sure things on her mind — The Cavity Ranger and his drill of fire scared her down to her peanut brittle bones, and she knew she had to run off the Range and climb up Marshmallow Mountain.

"Who can help me?" she thought. All of a sudden Jolene noticed a chubby lady sitting on a chunk of chocolate. Madame Fudge had dark brown, round eyes like Jolene's favorite chocolate chip cookies. She walked up to the lady. "Who are you?"

"I'm Madame Fudge. I will not budge. I will not budge a bit. If anybody takes my fudge, I'll simply have a fit," she squealed.

"I don't want your fudge, Madame, I just want to climb over that mountain," said Jolene.

Jolene had to cover her ears while Madame Fudge kept squealing like a pen full of potbelly pigs. "There's a spooky castle beyond the mountain and a bunch of strange and scary men live there. Be very careful, Jolene, and don't talk to the creepy creeps in the castle."

"I won't talk, but can I whisper?"

Madame Fudge flung her mouth wide open, and Jolene was surprised to see so many golden fudge fillings. "I only ate sixteen pieces of fudge today — sixteen more, and I'm on my way. Don't make my mistakes, Jolene. Hurry now and go before the mountain winds blow!"

Jolene waved to Madame Fudge as her shrinking voice echoed in the distance, "Good-bye, Madame Fudge! Good-bye, Madame Fudge!"

One at a time Jolene began bouncing over the marshmallows when suddenly her tummy began to grumble. A fuzzy snow bird flew up to her, dropping down a mug of hot chocolate with mini marshmallows. "Mmm, yummy," exclaimed Jolene. But she remembered The Cavity Ranger's warnings and only drank half the cup.

"When will I be there? This is taking forever," Jolene muttered. She rolled her eyes 'round and 'round and finally caught sight of the most ginormous castle in the world. *"I can't go in 'cause I promised Madame Fudge."*

Just then a magic strip of pink bubble gum unfolded, rolling toward Jolene. She stepped on it but couldn't move. "I'm stuck," she moaned. "I'm being gulped up by gum!"

The carpet of gum rolled up all around
Jolene when out popped two little gumball
buddies. The tiny tots unstuck Jolene from
the gummy carpet and stuffed her into a
tall, transparent tube that spun her
around and around like the revolving
door at the candy store.

When it stopped spinning, a speckled glass door popped open and spit Jolene out onto the ground without a trace of gooey gum on her.

"Who are you guys?" asked Jolene.

The gumball buddies were chewing and chomping, giggling and tumbling toward Jolene as they exclaimed, "We're The Bubblegummers! We just made you sticky-free!"

Jolene rubbed her hands together to feel her silky smooth skin. "Oh, thank you very much, but you made me really dizzy, too. Plus I'm so tired. I just bounced over Marshmallow Mountain, but that was like a fun trampoline!" beamed Jolene.

"Oh, come take a ride on our gumboline," said a Bubblegummer. "It's so much 'funner'!"

Jolene and The Bubblegummers bounced higher and higher on the gumboline and soon landed at the castle door.

"Let's go see Doctor-Do-Dye. He's super sweet, and he loves to invent the most candicious creations," boasted The Bubblegummers.

When the giant polka-dotted door creaked open, Jolene thought her eyes were playing bad tricks on her. She stared right into Doctor-Do-Dye's mouth and saw oodles of pink gums, no teeth! "What happened to all your teeth?" she asked.

Doctor-Do-Dye shot Jolene a bright pinky-pink smile. "Oh, it's from eating all my candy food. Would you like to try my terrific treats?"

"No, thank you!" said Jolene. She had never seen anyone like Doctor-Do-Dye before. His hair was purple, green, yellow, orange and red. It stuck straight above his head. He wore a stained pink sweater, and his glasses didn't look much better. He walked funny too, and his lips were neon blue.

"I pass out my samples all day long. My lab is loaded with orders to fill for my candy creations!" said the professor.

Jolene kept thinking about The Cavity Ranger as she entered the laboratory. She was amazed to see a gazillion liquid chemicals and crystal powders brewing and bubbling in their sugar-coated beakers.

Doctor-Do-Dye offered Jolene something that looked like a ham sandwich. "Try this tasty treat. It's nothing like meat."

"So what is it?" she asked.

"Why, it's my fake food made of sugar, dyes and a chemical surprise," explained the professor.

Jolene walked over to Doctor-Do-Dye and got in his face. "Why don't you use real fruit and veggies instead of all that goopy garbage and creepy chemicals?"

The professor handed Jolene a slip of sugar paper with a list of all the money he made from his candy food. "Kids love it and keep buying it. I need the money. I'm building my second castle in Hershey, Pennsylvania," said Doctor-Do-Dye.

Jolene turned bright candy apple red in the face. "That's bad cheating. If you used real food kids would be healthier."

Doctor-Do-Dye's candy machines were cranked up at such a high speed that all of a sudden one exploded in a BIG BAD BLAST! He vanished in a powerful puff of pink and purple smoke. So surprised was Jolene that she didn't hear the loud bells and whistles all around her. Then she saw two policemen rushing to the scene of the slime. One policeman had melted mozzarella cheese dripping to his knees, while the other one had a flat round disk on his right wrist. "Wow! That's a gigantic watch you're wearing."

The Pizza Police guy bent down so Jolene could see it better. "It's my Pizza Police watch. It tells the right time and that's why it's on my right wrist. We are The Pizza Police and we fight food crime. I'm Moe and he's Doe."

Jolene seemed confused. She had never heard of The Pizza Police although she loved pizza. "Are you here to give me a double pepperoni with cheese?" asked Jolene.

Doe rang the bell. "Well, you'll get part of a pizza, Jolene."

"We're here today to give you our official pepperoni bracelet," said Moe as he reached in his pocket and hand-tossed her the spicy bracelet.

Jolene was thrilled. Pepperoni pizza was her favorite food in the whole wide junk food world. She also liked bacon and sausage pizza. "I love this pepperoni bracelet," gushed Jolene. "Would you have another one for my friend, Sugar Sam?"

"Of course, Jolene, we have bracelets for all your friends, but only if you wear yours first," said Doe.

Jolene began bouncing up and down. "Oh yes I will!"

Moe wrapped the pepperoni bracelet around Jolene's wrist. "I must warn you, this piece of pepperoni will start to sizzle soon."

"How hot will it get?" asked Jolene.

Moe let out some steam. "It has to broil till it's golden brown to do the trick. This Pizza Police watch will let us know when the bracelet's well done. Here's the thing, Jolene. You eat too many pepperoni, bacon and sausage pizzas. We hear you eat them for breakfast, lunch and dinner too. This bracelet will de-pepperonize you from head to toe so you will be nitrate free."

Jolene shook her wrist to loosen the broiling bracelet. "I want this bracelet off now! This is a cheesy trick. I love my pizza. I never even heard of nitrates. They must be from science class. Yucky! Yuck!"

When Doe saw Jolene's sad face, he said, "I've got a double-crust idea. Let's all go visit Phantom of the French Fries. He doesn't get out much."

"He must be a couch potato," grinned Jolene with a twinkie in her eye.

Moe smiled as he led the way. "Follow us now, Jolene, into The Phantom's chambers."

"I love my French fries so much. I eat 115 fries a day. They keep The Munch Bunch away," said Jolene as she slipped through the greasy chamber doors.

The Phantom of the French Fries was delighted to see his guests. He slid up from his ketchup-covered desk. Jolene stood perfectly still, amazed at The Phantom's long shoestring fingers shaped just like her favorite fries. Jolene's eyes followed his flowing crimson cape as he approached her.

"Allow me to introduce myself. I am Phantom of the French Fries, and you must be little Jolene, The Junk Food Queen."

Jolene slowly crept up to Phantom of the French Fries. She put both hands on her hips like grown-up ladies do when they're mad at something. "I'm not so little, Mr. Phantom. You just happen to be a giant with big fat French fry fingers!"

Upon hearing Jolene's words, The Phantom's hands began to tremble. "Please, don't call me names. That hurts my SUPER-SIZE feelings. I'm just a big sensitive spud, you know."

Jolene kept staring at The Phantom's greasy gross French fry fingers dripping with red ketchup. "Can you make them go away? They're scaring me."

Phantom of the French Fries slipped his hideous hands into his velvet pockets. "They sadly will never go away, Jolene. The worst part of it is, they are constantly dripping ketchup on my lovely castle carpet," he said. "I do have a secret for you, Jolene. Listen carefully to me and you can beat the grease piece by piece."

Jolene's eyes lit up with excitement. "Oh, I love secrets. I tell them all the time back home, but I won't tell anyone here, Mr. Phantom — I pinky promise." Jolene walked up to Phantom of the French Fries. "Give me a French fry high-five!"

The Phantom high-fived Jolene's little hand, covering it with sloppy-gloppy ketchup. Suddenly a loud alarm rang that made Jolene jump.

Moe announced that de-pepperonization time was up, and declared the bracelet must come off right away! The Pizza Police hand-tossed the key to Jolene, and she unlocked the pepperoni stick bracelet. "Congratulations, you are now bad-chemical free! How does it feel?"

Jolene rubbed her right wrist. "I feel exactly the same. I'm still going to eat my pepperoni pizzas. I've lost trust in your crust!"

"Let's come up with a new plan," said Phantom of the French Fries as he tapped his greasy fingers on his desk. "Now, where were we?" He picked up his French fry calculator and pointed to his French fry chart as Jolene stared at his doodles.

"So, Jolene, I've calculated you eat over 800 French fries every week. Way too much grease! Listen closely to my new math," slobbered The Phantom. "If you cut down and eat only 50 fries a week, you won't have to worry about growing French fry fingers like mine."

Jolene leaped up with a jolt and pounded her hands on the desk. "I could never eat just 50 fries a week! One full order at The Potato Sack Shack is a catrillion tons of fries, and my Aunt knows the owner, so *I* get a catrillion *more* tons of fries!"

Phantom of the French Fries kept pointing to his chart. "I'm concerned about the grease factor, Jolene. Five ounces of fries gives you 542 calories of fat and loads of salt. I've done my homework. I'm a greaseologist," bragged The Phantom.

He then boldly banged his French fry stick against the chart. "I study the fat in fries and cut right to the grease. Since you eat too many fries, Jolene, you will soon turn into a mini me."

Jolene made a fan with her fingers over her face and started to cry. The Pizza Police heard Jolene whimpering and rushed over with a half-baked idea. "Let's put the fries in the oven and call them 'stove sticks'," said Doe.

"You guys are all weird and scary with your burning bracelets and French fry formulas. Maybe if you used nicer ways, I might eat junk food only on Fridays."

The Phantom waved his French fry fingers over a crystal ball sitting on his ketchup-coated desk. "Nicer ways aren't always better ways," declared The Phantom. "I see that your future isn't going to be sugar-coated anymore. That was the clue I was looking for, Jolene. You see this is not working out like I

planned. I am going to send you to The Goody Kingdom where you can find some new choices, some better ways, and say good-bye to those junk food days. Do you follow me, Jolene?"

"No, I don't follow you. I've heard enough of your stupid stuff! The only way I want to go is back home."

As Jolene jumped up to leave, a double-time chime announced the arrival of a new visitor.

Pizza Police Moe sprung open the chamber doors. "The Salad Heads are here!"

Salad Head Fred and Salad Head Ted bounced into The Phantom's chambers. "Hi, Jolene! I'm Salad Head Fred and this is my cousin Ted. We're here to tell you about the cool new scene at The Goody Kingdom."

"We heard some juicy bits of gossip that you're starting your salad days," said Ted as he did a cartwheel over Jolene's licorice head. "When we take you to our salad bar, you'll become a veggie star! Just bring your appetite...it's a real treat delight! One night at The Goody Kingdom and you'll sleep tight forever."

"Wow, you talk really fast. Where do you get all that energy?" Jolene asked.

Salad Head Fred started tossing his head back and forth. "It's called Greenergy! That's from all the awesome green foods I eat. They make me a totally action-packed, super-hero salad head! Watch me flex my muscles."

Jolene squeezed Salad Head Fred's arm and felt his green power. "Ooh, you're just like 'The Terminator' back home!"

"Remember my Greenergy. You can get some too!" said Salad Head Fred. "We'd better be on our way. Good-bye Pizza Police, good-bye Phantom. We'll take good care of Jolene. She needs a new scene! We hope she'll turn over a new leaf now."

Salad Head Fred held Jolene's hand as they bounced out the castle doors to a shiny golden draw bridge. They crossed the bridge and soon entered a forest-like neighborhood.

"Now this is more like home," said Jolene as she and The Salad Heads reached a maple syrup log cabin with a quilted sign that spelled out "Welcome to The Goody Kingdom."

"This feels like a happy place," said Jolene. "I love the smiling and singing and dancing. What a cool band. What's their name?"

"Those big bushy stalks are The Broccoli Bears, and The Corn Kernels are bopping and popping to the beat," said Salad Head Ted as they walked into the bright and busy world of The Kingdom.

"Who are they?" asked Jolene as she pointed to a group of girls in colorful clothes and funky hair-dos.

"We're The Blender Babes — Peaches, Kiwi and Berri."

They all seemed to talk at the same time. Kiwi wore bright green capris, Berri wore super-styling tees, and Peaches wore an orange skirt that crossed her knees.

"Why are your cheeks so pretty pink?" asked Jolene.

"We juice fresh fruit blends every day and drink them right away. They're the sweetest smoothies in The Goody Kingdom."

Peaches walked up to Jolene and held out her cheek. "Feel my peaches and cream complexion. It's super soft and smooth."

"Wow, that's even softer than my Taffy's tummy," said Jolene.

"Would you like to make some fruit smoothies with us, Jolene?" asked The Blender Babes. "It's as easy as pie but much better for you."

"Excuse me, Blender Babes, but what exactly is a smoothie?"

"It's a smooth and creamy drink," said The Babes. "You'll love sipping them all day long, and they will make you super-strong. Smoothies have real organic fruit that's sweet and yummy so only pureness goes in your tummy. We put goodies in our blenders and shake them twice. We add crushed ice to make them nice. After we shake, then we blend, and we end with milk of almond, soy or rice. The fresh fruit comes from paradise."

"Life's just a bowl of blueberries, strawberries and boysen-berries," said Berri. "Now follow us, Jolene, to Smoothie Central in The Goody Kingdom, where you can see the real action!"

When Jolene entered Smoothie Central she was amazed at the millions of mounds of fresh fruit in pink, green and blue baskets, and rows and rows of blenders whirling and swirling all at once. Peaches handed Jolene a tall tumbler frothing to the top like creamy orange bubble bath. "Try it."

Jolene took a tiny sip, then a bigger one, then a super slurp. "I love it!" exclaimed Jolene. "It tastes like ice cream, but better."

"It's called 'the works,' and it has juicy bits of all of us in it. We mix it up with kiwi, berries and peaches."

Pretty soon Jolene was blending her own fruit treats like a Smoothie Queen. She made rainbow smoothies of peaches and cream, a banana dream and a berry supreme. They all tasted great, but her favorite was a red, white and blue triple ice skate. She mixed in blueberries, strawberries, raspberries, three chunks of ice, a scoop of yoghurt, and created a super delight.

"Are you ready for our sampling party?" The Blender Babes asked.

"What are we going to sample?"

"Oh, Jolene, wait till you see what treats are ahead. You'll just love them!" said Blender Babe Kiwi. "We've invited our friends Bella Pepper and the boxing team, The Fighting Figs, to join in the fun. The Broccoli Bears made their favorite dips, we made our blender drinks, and Ted and Fred piled up sky-high salads."

Jolene's eyes opened wider than the sparkly pink plate Berri handed her. "That sounds really yummy. Sure, I'll try some."

The Broccoli Bears began playing their music. The Salad Heads did cartwheels and head stands, and The Blender Babes whirled and twirled.

When the clock struck 6 p.m., Bella Pepper and The Fighting Figs dropped in. Then a loud bell rang to announce the beginning of the sampling party. The room was filled with tree trunk tables and lemon lanterns. A colorful piñata stuffed with toys was on display above the food buffet.

"Hey, Broccoli Bear Bill, this artichoke dip is pretty good," said Jolene.

"Thanks a bunch! I whipped up tasty things with ease — veggies and seeds and spices to please."

The Salad Heads were busy dicing and slicing, shredding and tossing when Jolene pushed her plate in front of them. "May I try some?"

"Of course," said Salad Head Fred.

She piled on her plate red cabbage, spinach, carrots, corn and chick peas, pasta, pumpkin seeds and little broccoli trees.

"Now let's put on my special dressing to make your salad *Zing-A-Ling-A-Ling*!" Salad Head Fred blended a little olive oil, apple cider vinegar, lemon and lime, salt and pepper, and it was simply divine.

Jolene started eating her salad and soon cleaned the whole plate down to its last sparkly spot. "You know what, guys? I really like salads!"

No one could believe what they heard. Everyone gathered around Jolene and asked her to repeat it. Jolene yelled at the top of her voice, "I love salads!"

They all shouted back, "Hoorah, she loves salads!"

In all the excitement, The Salad Heads got everyone tossing and shaking while The Broccoli Bears' band blasted at a high, happy pitch.

Bella Pepper began to dance the Spicy Salsa, and The Fighting Figs sweated up a storm.

Then Blender Babe Berri twirled Jolene 'round and 'round like a carrot top till they finally sat down.

"This is the last time I will see you. Remember, one night in The Goody Kingdom does the trick. When you wake up tomorrow, you'll be home again," said Blender Babe Berri.

Peaches and Kiwi came over to give Jolene a warm and fuzzy hug.

"I'm going to miss all my new friends," said Jolene. "I had so much fun, and now I have so much good stuff in me."

"Here, this is especially for you," said Kiwi as she handed Jolene a shiny book with pink, yellow and green glittery pages called *The Blender Babes Gone Bananas.* "They're recipes of our yummiest smoothies so you can blend with your friends back home."

"And this is from us," said Broccoli Bear Bill. "It's a CD of our favorite songs, called 'Green Ambition — The Broccoli Bears Live in Concert'."

Jolene began rubbing her eyes. "Thanks for the really cool presents, but all this sampling fun has made me a sleepy-head."

Ted and Fred took Jolene to her salad bed. "Lay down on this soft mattress stuffed with shredded cabbage, put these cucumber slices on your eyes, baby corn cobs in your ears for plugs, and cover up with fresh leaves of lettuce."

Jolene climbed into her salad bed and pulled the bib lettuce blanket over her head. "Good night Berri, good night Kiwi, good night Peaches, good night Ted, good night Fred, good night Broccoli Bears."

"Good night, Jolene. Sweet smoothie dreams."

Thinking about The Goody Kingdom and all her exciting adventures, Jolene fell into a deep sleep. She slowly opened her eyes and realized she was back home again. As she jumped out of bed she gave cuddly hugs to Bubba and Taffy and was happy to start a big new day.

Jolene rushed over to her closet and picked out a pretty white dress with matching hair bows and tennis shoes. Then she ran out to the bright orange kitchen. She crept up behind her mom and surprised her with big, juicy kisses. *Smack, smack, smack.* "Mom, I don't want my junk food lunch today. I want that other healthy stuff you always make."

Jolene's Mom stared at her in a super-glazed way just like Jolene's favorite doughnuts. "I can't believe my ears! Am I dreaming? No more junk food junkies? *I'm so proud of you, Jolene!*" exclaimed her mother. "Let's start our day with a brand new breakfast. How about some yummy fruit and granola instead of your yucky candy and cola? Let's finish with a pineapple freeze topped with mint leaves."

After eating her new breakfast, Jolene dashed out the door
to catch the big yellow bus. As she climbed on the bus all The
Munch Bunch began to whisper.

Tracy was the first one to speak. "Jolene, you look so different.
Where's your jelly bean boots and jean jacket with lollipop hoops?
Are you trying to trick us?"

Jolene's cheeks blushed and flushed from all the attention.
"Oh, I had this delicious dream, and now I'm so healthy I could
scream!"

The Munch Bunch banged their shoes on the back of the bus
seats and shouted, "No way! She's gone organic. Do we need to
panic? Way to go, Jolene! Good-bye, Junk Food Queen."

Suddenly everyone wanted to be Jolene's friend. Hannah started telling Jolene all about Sugar Sam. "He put a pile of gummy worms on the teacher's chair. After that he poured his candy powder all over the floor and spit on it. Gross! And then super-gross when he licked his green sucker and stuck it in Rosie's hair. He got a big time-out. He might have to leave school. Maybe you could help him, Jolene."

In art class Jolene thought about her dream and how she could change Sugar Sam. She walked over to her friend Tracy who was splashed and splattered from head to toe in pink paint.

"Look, Jolene, I'm Pinkasso!"

Jolene took Tracy's paint brush and spelled out the name — Sugar Sam. "I have a cool plan. Let's go deep into the dark and dense forest where Sugar Sam's house is crawling with gummy worms. We can ask Mrs. Sweet if he can come to my spring break party. We'll only have healthy foods there, and Sugar Sam will have to eat them."

"What if we lock Sugar Sam in candy jail? He would only eat candy — candy for breakfast, candy for lunch, candy for dinner and candy for snacks. Sugar Sam will get so sick of candy he'll never want to see it again."

"No way, Tracy. Sugar Sam can't learn healthy eating that way. He may love candy jail so much he'll never want to come out."

Tracy walked with Jolene down the mostly muddy path leading to the dark purple forest where they heard the music of The Three Wise Wolves. Their tropical tunes echoed throughout the vast forest.

The Three Wise Wolves always had samples of fresh fruits and vegetables at their stands and offered some to Jolene and Tracy. Jolene told the wolves that they were headed to Sugar Sam's house.

One of the Wise Wolves wore a sulky, sad expression. "Ooh, you're going to that Sugar Shack. That mom never gives us any business. She only feeds Sugar Sam candy. She's just like her sister, Missy Sour Grapes."

Jolene seemed surprised. "Oh no, you're wrong. They may be sugar sisters, but Mrs. Sweet is super sweet and Missy Sour Grapes is super sour." Jolene turned around, and when she saw the sour sister walking her way, she suddenly felt like her heart was going to pop out of her chest! Missy Sour Grapes wore a purple powdered-sugar dress with sour grape candies draped around her neck. Her curly hair glistened like glitter from purple fizzy powder.

Missy Sour Grapes stepped on Jolene's toes, trying to squeeze and squish them. "I've heard about you, Jolene. You're no longer a Junk Food Queen. I hope that means you still eat some sugar. I am The Sour Grape Candy Queen, and this purple forest will never be pink and green."

Jolene almost choked on her mouthful of blueberries. "Well, this forest should be pink and green — it should be healthy and clean!"

Missy Sour Grapes laughed deep and loud. "It will never be that scene, Jolene. My magic grape stick does the trick. You and your words make me sick." Missy Sour Grapes then pushed a button on her grape stick and sour candies came squirting out. "I'm on my way. Have a sour grape day!"

Jolene's cheeks turned purply red with rage. "I'm going to bring her down. I don't like her ugly frown. I've heard it through the grapevine that the stick has a code that can turn her into grape jelly."

Tracy clapped her hands. "Yes, it's true! I've heard it too! Here's what we have to do. We have to go to her sour grape cabin and crack the code."

Jolene and Tracy finished gobbling up a bunch of berries and promised the wolves they'd get the job done. "We're going to change Sugar Sam," announced Jolene, "and then turn the forest pink and green."

The first Wise Wolf gazed at Jolene and Tracy in disbelief. "Good luck, and be careful. That mean Missy Sour Grapes is a real purple fizzy witch."

The second Wise Wolf handed the girls his new mail order catalogue. "I'm having a bad eggplant year. Pass these out to your friends so my fruit and veggie sales will grow."

The third Wise Wolf gave Jolene and Tracy a basket of fresh fruit. "Take this to your moms for doing such a plum job in raising a hearty crop of girls."

They thanked the wolves and ran off as fast as they could through the soft purple mud. Sugar Sam's candy cabin was made of sparkling white sugar cubes, and covered in giant-sized lollipops and bite-sized candy drops. Jolene rang the large cinnamon bun door bell. Mrs. Sweet opened the door and was surprised to see the girls. "Jolene, where are your cute little candy clothes?"

"Oh, they went out of style — stale in fact, Mrs. Sweet." Jolene glanced around the house. The floors were made of sugar cane planks with crates of candy scattered all around.

"Where's Sugar Sam?" asked Tracy as a clingy candy wrapper snagged her sneaker.

Mrs. Sweet began shouting his name. "Oh fudge, I forgot. He has a lollipop stuck in his hair and he's trying to unstick it."

Sugar Sam finally came out to greet his friends. Since his giant green lollipop still tugged on a big chunk of hair, it seemed like his head was leaning to one side.

Jolene giggled. "Sugar Sam, you're like the trees in the purple forest. They lean to the left just like your head!"

Tracy helped Sugar Sam yank the lopsided lollipop out of his hair. "Ouch! Ouch! Ouch!" screamed Sugar Sam.

"That's what you'd call a bad hair day," said Tracy. She handed him an invitation to their party.

"We are going to have so much fun! You have to come," shouted Jolene.

"Sure I'll come, but only if I can bring my favorite candy," said Sugar Sam.

"That would be rude," said Jolene. "And yucky."

Mrs. Sweet offered the girls some of her special sugar cookies. Jolene had one tempting taste. "Thank you, Mrs. Sweet. Your cookies are the best, but I should only have one big bite. One big bite is all right."

The girls waved good-bye to Sugar Sam and Mrs. Sweet as they skipped along the purple path to Missy Sour Grapes's cabin in the forest. It was covered in sour grape candy kisses, and the girls heard purple snake hisses as they tip-toed up to the sugar pane window.

"Look, she's sleeping, but I don't see the grape stick," said Tracy.

Jolene glanced up — hanging on a hook on top of the window ledge was the grape stick. Jolene jumped once, twice, three times and grabbed the stick in her hand. "I got it!"

"Good job, Jolene. Now what about the secret code?"

"Sugar Sam spilled the jelly beans one day and told me the un-secret code."

The girls noticed Missy Sour Grapes snoring and roaring in her sleep. "Hurry before one of the purple snakes bites us or Missy Sour Grapes bites our heads off," moaned Tracy.

Jolene punched the code on the grape stick as she chanted out loud, "Sugar rules! Purple rocks! It'll knock you off your socks!"

Suddenly the purple ground beneath them began jiggling and wiggling with pink and green lights flashing on and off. Everything went perfectly quiet, still and black. When the lights beamed back on, Jolene and Tracy began spinning around while twinkly white lights lit up the ground. The entire purple forest morphed into an enchanted land with rows and rows of pink peonies, green apple trees and honey bees. In the distance, Mrs. Sweet's Sugar Shack could be seen. Everything about it was pink and green. Missy Sour Grapes's cabin was sparkling pink, too. A big blob of grape jelly sat as a door mat.

"It could be poison. Don't touch it," warned Tracy.

Jolene didn't care. She kicked off her shoes and jumped into the purple jelly blob squishing her feet deeper and deeper. "It's so yucky and gooey!" squealed Jolene. "I'm finished with the sugar scene."

Jolene and Tracy buzzed around the new flower beds. "This is better than a dream. The purple forest is now pink and green. Let's go, Jolene."

"I have a great idea," said Jolene. "We can have a planting party right here in the new fresh forest."

As the girls hurried home, they decided to keep the magic of the purple forest a secret for a little while. All they could think about was the party.

"Let's make smoothies," suggested Jolene.

The Munch Bunch had some fun food ideas too. "How about turkey chili burgers?" said Stephie.

"Let's have organic almond butter and banana chips," exclaimed Tracy.

"I like whole wheat waffles with pure maple syrup," chimed in Marni.

"Have you ever tried a veggie pizza?" asked Alexandra.

The party lasted the whole spring break. Jolene's mom kept a close eye on Sugar Sam. "He's having the sugar shakes since he hasn't eaten candy in a week."

"Y'know, he's not good at school. He always makes bad grades," whispered Kelly.

Jolene's mom explained to the girls how Sugar Sam eats two pounds of sugar a week. She told them that when the sugar goes into his blood, his brain goes foggy and his grades crash. "He can't remember what he's learning from all that sugar on the brain."

Each day Sugar Sam would beg and cry for candy. "Where are all the sweet snacks?"

Jolene or another Munch Buncher always gave Sugar Sam trail mix, soy burgers or veggie chips instead. Jolene blended fresh fruit smoothies too. By the second week Sugar Sam was doing great. He had a ton of energy and his cheeks suddenly turned bright pink.

Jolene and Tracy cut off all his candy hair and gave him new clothes to wear.

"You look so good now, Sam. We did it because we are your friends," said Jolene.

Sam began doing somersaults and flips, skipping rope and other neat tricks, showing off to the girls. "I wish I could go back to a healthy home," he said.

Jolene shouted, "You can — you will! Tracy and I have a big surprise. We changed the dark purple forest and made it healthy. I'm having a big planting party there tomorrow!"

The Munch Bunch was so excited to see the new un-purple forest. One by one, Jolene gave her friends their planting packets.

"It's pink and green. It's a brand new scene!" exclaimed Tina.

Ooh's and ahh's were heard everywhere. No one could believe their eyes.

Mrs. Sweet brought planting tools for everyone. "I'm a health food lover now. My house is full of fruits and veggies!"

Mrs. Sweet planted sweet potatoes and sugar snap peas. Ariel planted artichokes. Brett planted beets. Carrie planted carrots. Dustin planted dates. Emma planted eggplant. Fern planted figs. Gina and Griffin planted green beans. Hannah planted herbs. Isabel planted Italian squash. Jolene planted jicama. Kelly planted kumquats. Lauren planted lettuce. Marni planted melons. Natalie planted nectarines. Olivia planted olives. Parker planted parsnips. Quinn planted quinoa. Rosie planted radishes. Stephie planted spinach. Tracy and Tina planted turnips. Ursula planted ugli fruit that was really quite pretty.

Victoria planted a variety of vegetables. William planted watermelon. Xavier with his extra-special green thumb helped all his friends plant their seeds. Yale planted yams. Finally, Zoie planted zucchini.

Everyone had fun at Jolene's planting party except Jolene. "I'm worried that some day my junk food dreams might come back. What will I do then?"

"Uhh-uhh, no way, Jolene. You've crossed over Junk Food Street, and you'll never go back," said Alexandra.

Jolene dug her shovel into the ground. "You're right, Alexandra, I'm not a Junk Food Queen anymore — I'm a Health Food Queen. And besides, I can always eat a little bit of junk food on Fridays."

"Just as long as you don't eat a triple hunormous bite," said The Munch Bunch.

"Don't forget your Salad Days, Jolene!"

"The Cavity Ranger rocks!"

"The Pizza Police sizzle!"

"The Blender Babes rule!"

"The Broccoli Bears forever!"

"Deal!" shouted The Munch Bunch.

"Deal!" shouted back Jolene.

They all sealed the deal with high-fives and smoothies.

Jolene's Favorite Smoothie Recipes

(From *The Blender Babes Gone Bananas*)

Bonanza Berry Brain-Freeze Blast

Makes 2 — one for you and one for a friend

1 humungo frozen banana (it has real appeal)

1 grown-up handful or 2 kid-handfuls of fresh or frozen blueberries

1 cup of almond, soy, rice or hazelnut milk (your mom, dad or other big person will be able to find these in the supermarket)

1 ginormous chunk of ice

1 small spoon of honey

Get a grown-up to help you put all these yummy ingredients in a blender and whirl, twirl and swirl them until creamy and smooth. Serve in a cool-looking cup with a crazy straw if you want to go bananas.

Mango Tango Meltdown

1 ripe mango, peeled and chopped into chunks (or just take one grown-up or 2 kid-handfuls of frozen mango chunks)

1/2 cup of orange juice

1/2 cup of super thick vanilla yogurt

1 teaspoon of honey

Once again, have a grown-up help you put all these ingredients in a blender and whirl, twirl and swirl them until creamy. Pour this into a fun cup with a cool straw and sip away.

Peanut-Butter-and-Jelly Outside-the-Sandwich Smoothie

2 huge spoonfuls of peanut butter or almond butter, which is even better
    (organic is best since it doesn't have bad chemicals in it)
1 big spoonful of your favorite jam or jelly (the all-fruit kind is awesome)
2 cups of almond, soy, rice or hazelnut milk
1 chunk of ice

By now you're a smoothie expert! You can help the grown-up smoothie maker
put all these ingredients in a blender and whirl, twirl and swirl them until
smooth. Put this in a colorful cup (not in a sandwich!) and slurp it up for
breakfast, lunch or snack time.

Have a smoothie sampling party with your best friends and new friends!

The Scoop on Smoothies

Smoothies were around long before Jolene was born.

Many years ago, a young man named Steve discovered that he got terrible tummy aches when he drank milkshakes. He worked in a soda fountain shop, so he decided to create yummy drinks without milk. He called these frozen drink treats "smoothies." People liked Steve's smoothies so much, he became known as "The Smoothie King." This gave him an idea: He would open smoothie fountains all over the country, and he'd call his company—and each one of his stores—'The Smoothie King.'

His chain of stores became a huge hit. Smoothies captured children's taste buds right from the beginning. Kids especially loved creating their own by pointing at the different colorful fruits behind the glass and asking, "Please, put this one in! Put that one in, too!" Their parents also loved these thick and refreshing drinks for their flavors—but also because they had lots of fresh vitamins in them that helped make everyone stronger and healthier.

Nowadays, you can buy smoothies at many different shops, but still the creamiest, dreamiest, freshest ones can be whirled, twirled and swirled in the blender in your own home.

CPSIA information can be obtained at www.ICGtesting.com
Printed in the USA
BVIW12n2030040815
411785BV00001B/1

* 9 7 8 0 6 1 5 1 3 6 3 0 1 *